D1274845

Corgi and Bess

Corgi and Bess

MORE WIT AND WISDOM FROM
THE HOUSE OF WINDSOR

THOMAS BLAIKIE

FOURTH ESTATE • London

First published in Great Britain in 2006 by
Fourth Estate
An imprint of HarperCollins*Publishers*
77–85 Fulham Palace Road
London w6 8jb
www.4thestate.co.uk

2

A catalogue record for this book is
available from the British Library

ISBN-13 978-0-00-724110-1
ISBN-10 0-00-724110-0

Set in Linotype Minion by
Rowland Phototypesetting Ltd, Bury St Edmunds, Suffolk

Printed in Great Britain by Clays Ltd, St Ives plc

Acknowledgements

Many thanks to the following for their generous support of the tiresome author. Some suggested helpful leads in the arduous search for Royal stories and others kindly gave me raw material for this book: Tom Adès, Juliet Annan, Tash Aw, Adam Bager, Paul Bailey, Miles Barber, Nadine Baylis, Emma Beale, Tamsyn Blaikie, Michael Bloch, Sarah Bradford, Gyles Brandreth, Harry Bucknall, Angus Canvin, Miranda Carter, Sam Clark, John Clinch, Jilly Cooper, Caroline Dashwood, Stephen de Silva, Odile Ellis, Peter Eyre, Annette Fynes-Clinton, Derek Granger, Charlie Gurdon, Bill Hamilton, Nicky Haslam, Ian Hay, Gregory Hayman, Alan Hollinghurst, Tim Hely Hutchinson, Alastair Hendy, Philip Hensher, Brian Hoey, Joe Hunter, Magdalen Jebb, Wesley Kerr, Jeremy Lawrence, Sarah Long, Katharine MacDonogh, Abigail Manning, Jean-Bernard Marie, Rick Mather, Kitty Morris, John Julius Norwich, Patrick O'Connor, Peter Parker, Kate Parkin, Kenneth Partridge, Sarah Patterson,

Christopher Potter, Sean Rafferty, Kit Reading, Kenneth Rose, Hilary Rossington, Lord St John of Fawsley, Tony Scotland, David Scrace, Ivan Seery, Jane Seery, Nigel Spalding, Humphrey Stone, Sir Roy Strong, Sean Swallow, Christopher Thorne, Petroc Trelawny, Richard Walker, Anthony Wilson, J. H. G. Woollcombe CBE, Phoebe Woollcombe, Susan Woollcombe, Magdalen Woollcombe-Gosson.

Special thanks to Silvia Crompton of Fourth Estate for her calm efficiency, good sense and expert editorial eye.

Contents

Contents

Introduction

You Look Awfully Like the Queen, my previous collection of Royal stories, was my first book. For me, it was thrilling enough just to be published. It never occurred to me that anyone might buy the book or that sales might even be necessary.

But fortunately many of you did buy it, and in quite large numbers.

Informal, behind-the-scenes glimpses of Royal life, sometimes quirky (for the Windsors are *odd*, as you might expect), not always as fawningly flattering as old-fashioned deference would have demanded, but always affectionate, seem to be popular. Perhaps it is that they catch the spirit of the modern, more cheerful and friendly Monarchy which we all want and in fact have – for the Queen and the Monarchy *have* changed, despite all claims and appearance to the contrary. Gratifyingly for me, members of the Royal Family have taken to telling Royal anecdotes themselves. To mark his mother's 80th birthday, Prince Andrew gave a number of interviews in which he retold the title story of *You Look Awfully Like the Queen*, getting it slightly wrong, if I may say so.

Here, in *Corgi and Bess*, you will find many tantalising vignettes, the majority of them never before published or from elusive sources, of all the peculiar, contradictory traits of Royalty. One minute they are just like us, worrying about the shabby state of the curtains, and the next doing something really quite strange, like kissing a small child goodnight with a crown on or showing astonishing knowledge of the smoking habits of goats. You will find yourself experiencing, perhaps, equally contradictory feelings about them, veering from anxiety as to exactly how seriously to take them to respect and admiration.

You will see also changes in the Royal Family reflected. There are a number of exclusive stories about the Duchess of Cornwall, as well as Princes William and Harry. It is interesting that Princess Margaret, a few years after her death, begins to look less and less . . . well, I hesitate to say this . . . *awful*. Her idea was that there was no point in being a Princess unless you could do exactly as you liked – and that's just what she did, with breathtaking dash and aplomb. You've got to give it to her.

Royal anecdotes may be popular but that doesn't mean they're easy to come by. No, they are *rare*. People who know them guard them jealously. I could write another whole book about the struggle I've had to excavate the stories in this one; but I was fortunate to come across some highly exclusive sources without, I can honestly say, having to penetrate the Palace disguised as a footman.

But in one maddening instance no amount of digging could achieve anything. Somebody told me a story about the Queen walking her dogs and meeting a member of the public who didn't recognise her (this could be true if it happened some time ago). This person had the cheek to suggest that the Queen's dogs were badly behaved and she ought to do something about it. Her Majesty made some funny reply, but my source *couldn't remember what it was*. Can you believe it?

So, if anyone thinks they know, do be in touch. I'm sure a suitable reward can be arranged.

Royal to the Core

'Royalty are marvellous – they never crease or stain.'

EVE POLLARD, *commenting on the fashions at Royal Ascot in the 1970s*

*I*n May 2006, the Queen was moved and delighted to open a garden in memory of Princess Margaret at Oxford's Rothermere American Institute. She had just one little reservation – the lettering on the plinth, was it big enough? She could hardly read her sister's name! Her hosts' explanation that maybe it was owing to the brightness of the day did not convince. On her way out, the Queen came across a poster for a student rock concert with outrageously bold lettering. 'That's the sort of thing you want,' she said.

Skinny-dipping in the River Dee on the Balmoral estate is a favourite pursuit of Royal staff and their guests. But it is very cold. You don't want to be in there for too long. Two young men cavorting in the river didn't think much of it when the Queen drew up on the bank in a Land Rover some years ago. She'd soon be gone and they could get out. But, sitting at the wheel, the Queen began to acquire an alarming regal immobility. She did not move. What's more, they formed the impression *she was doing it deliberately*. Only at the very last minute, when they really thought they could bear it no more and would be forced to leap naked from the water before their Sovereign, did the engine of the Land Rover splutter mercifully into life and the vehicle move off.

When, in the 1950s, Lady Pamela Berry came to inspect the arrangements for a fashion show to be attended by the Queen Mother and Princess Margaret, she said, 'What are these chairs?' refer- ring to two throne-like items which had been provided for the Royal persons. 'They won't do at all.' The organisers were put out. Lady Pamela Berry got the cleaning lady to sit in one of them. 'You see. Where are they to put their handbags? They can't go on the floor.' More capacious chairs with room to stow a handbag had to be found at once.

*A*t Eton Prince William came across a fellow-pupil throwing stones at a swan. 'Stop that, you ginga bastard!' he cried. 'Those are my granny's swans.' At Eton they don't say, 'ginger', they say, 'ginga'.

*P*rincess Margaret's journey from Kensington Palace to the Chelsea Flower Show (a distance of just over a mile) was accomplished under police escort in three and a half minutes.

*W*hen the Queen returned from her State Visit to China in the early 1980s, she arrived at Heathrow Airport at 8.48 in the evening. By 9.06 she was at the private entrance of Windsor Castle.

*D*uring the power cuts of the 1970s, the Queen sat at her desk, unperturbed and in the dark, wearing a mink coat.

*T*he Queen's private letters, marked ER in one corner, are sent by special messenger or registered post to help post-office workers resist the urge to make off with them.

*P*rince Charles has a way of dealing with smokers, which others might like to follow. 'Yes, of course,' he says, when someone asks if they may smoke, 'but I'm afraid there are no ashtrays.' Which leaves the would-be smoker nicely high and dry.

*E*very night for four weeks, in the run-up to Christmas, the Queen goes on a shopping spree in one of her own drawing rooms. A huge selection of goods, supplied by a certain London department store, is shipped in and displayed in her home shopping mall.

*I*n the days when the Queen spent Christmas at Windsor and then moved on immediately to Sandringham, all her Christmas cards, decorations and presents, including a menagerie of soft toys given her by Hardy Amies, went with her.

*T*he Queen takes no notice of the commonly held superstition that it is bad luck to keep your Christmas decorations up beyond Twelfth Night. Hers remain in place for as long as she feels like it.

*A*lthough in 2000 the Queen had to stay up to see in the New Year, century and millennium at Greenwich, at other times the Royal Family arranges things differently. Sometimes at ten o'clock on New Year's Eve a message is received in the kitchens: 'We want New Year now.' Staff rally round, altering all the clocks to suit.

$\mathcal{A}$ few years ago some old friends of the Queen living in North London invited her to their Golden Wedding party. They were delighted when it was announced at the last minute that she was actually coming but, since it was a private visit, it was explained that they would have to be responsible for the state of their garden path and front steps. No official inspection would be carried out beforehand. The Queen arrived, negotiating the steps without incident. But she could not be induced to sit down and, more importantly, could not be tempted near the fabulous buffet despite various children being propelled in her direction with winsome invitations. In the end, she said, 'I'd love to stay and have supper with you, but I've got so many boxes to do for tomorrow, I'll have to go home.' So off she went to a lonely working supper. At this time she was aged 75.

$\mathcal{P}$rincess Margaret may have liked to build up a huge fire in the drawing-room grate (anything combustible that came to hand might be flung on: hosts had to watch out), but she didn't greatly care for the warmth of human bodies near her. The composer Thomas Adès was once summoned by the Master of his Cambridge college to meet the Princess after dinner. He sat gingerly on a sofa with her, making charming conversation. Who knows, maybe he was enjoying himself just a little too much for suddenly the Princess was waving her hand dismissively: 'Could you move away? It's getting rather hot.' More waving indicated the far end of the sofa.

*P*rincess Margaret dined at Moro, the Sam Clarks' fabulous Moroccan-inspired restaurant in Clerkenwell, in 2000 after a grand Royal Ballet event at Sadler's Wells. Or rather, she didn't. She took one look at the glorious menu – pigeon *b'steeya* with almonds, sugar and cinnamon; wood-roast Middle White pork; and rosewater and cardamom ice-cream – and ordered a boiled egg.

*G*overnors and teachers were looking forward to lunch with Princess Margaret when she visited their school in the 1980s, especially since superior outside caterers had been engaged and they knew it wouldn't be the usual mince. But the Princess had her own unique way of expressing her disapproval of fine dining. At the end of the first course she rose to her feet and swept out of the room, leaving the others with no choice but to trot after her.

*N*icky Haslam recalls that, during a little marital disagreement, Princess Margaret became alarmed at Lord Snowdon's apparent carelessness with lighted matches. 'Watch out!' she said, 'you might set fire to my dress.' 'That wouldn't matter. I've never liked that material,' said Lord Snowdon. There was an unnerving pause, during which onlookers could hear the air stiffening as it froze. 'We call it *stuff*!' Princess Margaret boomed.

*A*fter meeting a British journalist during a Caribbean State Visit and discovering that he had had a surprise reunion with his own father during the Jamaican part of the tour, the Queen moved on to more important matters. 'And did he see me?' she inquired. 'Did he see me?'

*T*he actor Peter Eyre explained to Princess Margaret that he'd been on a march to protest about Clause 28 and that was why he was late for the party at Kathleen Tynan's they were both at. She said, 'I've no idea what you're talking about,' rising splendidly above politics, for Clause 28, as I'm sure you remember, was a piece of anti-gay legislation introduced by the Conservative Government in the 1980s. Peter Eyre, in rather belligerent mood, stuck to his guns. 'Are you sure you don't know?' he inquired. In the end, he said, 'It's about gay rights.' 'Oh, I see,' said Princess Margaret. 'Well, I do hope you all sang, "Tramp, Tramp, Tramp, the Boys Are Marching".'

*R*oyal bathrooms always feature three basins. To avoid confusion, they are labelled, 'teeth', 'hands' and 'face'.

*T*he Queen's outfits for the 1979 Gulf States visit were inspired by Marlene Dietrich in *Morocco*, a desert film in which she starred with Gary Cooper.

*T*he Queen Mother was possibly the only person to get through the entire 20th century without once having to draw or open her bedroom curtains herself.

*L*unching officially at the Savoy in 1994, the Queen Mother happened to be sitting next to one of her racing trainers, Nicky Henderson. Neither of them had been keeping an eye on the clock. Which was a mistake, as they wanted to catch the 3.10 at Fontwell Park and it was now 3.00. They'd better look sharp. The Queen Mother set off in her Rolls and the trainer followed behind in a taxi. They tore down the Strand, screeched through Trafalgar Square and then it was a clear, high-speed run to Clarence House. In at the front door, up the stairs, snap the set on – they were just in time. The Queen Mother was then 94.

*A*t Badminton during the War, Queen Mary said, 'So that's what hay looks like!' She was then aged 70.

*W*hen Princess Margaret was born, her father was all set to register the event at the Glamis post office when he noticed that the next slot in the book was Number 13. He thought he'd leave that for another baby and come back later. There was in fact a new-born but unregistered infant called George conveniently available for the purpose. His mother was told by the Glamis postmaster to come and register her child at once. She wasn't too keen to be Number 13 either but conceded that 'the Duchess was a charming person and spoke to us often as we cut through the Castle grounds on the way to church on Sundays'.

*D*uring the War, when some good folk who lived at the gates of Royal Lodge were badly bombed, their friends were most dismayed. But, rushing round to comfort and console, they found the pair in the best of spirits, indeed apparently buoyed up by the whole experience. It turned out the King and Queen had got there first. The husband was wearing one of the King's suits and the wife one of the Queen's dresses.

By ancient right the Lords Kingsdale are entitled to keep their hats on in the presence of the Sovereign. But the incumbent in Queen Victoria's time came unstuck when showily trying to exercise his privilege. The tiny Queen glared at him and his hat for a good while. 'We are also a lady,' she said eventually, putting a stop to this nonsense once and for all.

Staying at Badminton during the War, Queen Mary took up with a little dog (dogs had never before been her scene). She used to feed it a dog biscuit in some state after dinner each night. Once an elderly bishop was dining and Queen Mary passed on to him this responsibility. But the cleric was deaf. Clearly he thought he was being asked to undergo some curious Royal test; refusal was out of the question. He ate the biscuit himself.

At a garden party on a sunny day, Queen Mary wore so many diamonds she became just a blaze of white light, not really distinguishable as a person. One evening she wore five diamond necklaces, and a miffed lady remarked, 'She's bagged the lot.'

*F*or a routine visit to the East End in the morning, Queen Mary wore pale green lamé and emeralds.

*S*hattered by the relentlessness of Court life, especially the endless standing, Queen Victoria's doctor fainted dead away after dinner one day. 'And a doctor too,' was the Queen's only comment. Harsh but fair.

*I*n the 1950s, the Queen Mother took control of a Comet during a test-flight and put her foot down so hard on the accelerator that the plane began to porpoise. She was thrilled although she did acknowledge the other passengers might not have been. Later on, when Comets began mysteriously to crash and the phenomenon of metal fatigue was discovered, the Chairman of BOAC always recalled this flight with horror.

*D*uring the War, the Queen Mother, then Queen, learned to use a revolver, so that, should the Germans come after her, she could resist. 'I won't go down like the others,' she told Harold Nicolson, referring to all her weedy Royal colleagues, who had run away rather than face the enemy. Lord Halifax, the Foreign Secretary, who by special arrangement walked through the grounds of Buckingham Palace every morning on his way to work, was alarmed that the gardens seemed to be alive with the sound of gunfire. 'It is the Queen's target practice,' he was told. He decided to go by another route.

The Prince of Wales isn't extravagant. He just doesn't have any idea about money. He once asked if £40,000 were a lot to spend on a table. This was in the early 1990s. Somebody sensibly replied, 'It depends on the table.' To the suggestion that he might economise by raiding his mother's vast store of spare furniture, he responded, 'Oh, no, she won't part with a stick.'

Part of the 1977 Jubilee celebrations involved a late-night fireworks display on the Thames followed by an appearance of the Royal Family on the Buckingham Palace balcony. After this, the Queen Mother, then aged 77, wanted to go to bed. Clarence House being only a few hundred yards away, there should have been no difficulty. But the crowds around the Palace were

impenetrable. She was shut in. The police advised her to wait. But that, she declared, was out of the question. And who can blame her? She was after all Queen Dowager and last Empress of India. So she set off and the end of it all was that her car had to thread its way along a vastly circuitous route and it took 45 minutes to get back home. When at last, rather steamed up, she was inside the front door, she said, 'That was most pusillanimous.'

*A*t Eton, pupils taking A level History of Art were encouraged to develop their personal enthusiasms when it came to choosing a topic for the special project which is a required part of the course. 'I know,' said Prince William. 'I'll do Leonardo da Vinci's drawings.' This was a good choice and practical too, since most of the drawings are in his granny's collection at Windsor Castle.

*F*or Christmas 2002, Princes William and Harry received from their father – among other things, one hopes – a silk top hat apiece, acquired from Lock & Co. of St James at a cost of £1,200 each.

*V*isitors to Badminton in the 1980s were mystified by the sudden appearance of a mean little strip of carpet running up one side of the stairs. It turned out that, on her last visit, the Queen Mother had said, 'Unless you do something about those treacherous bare stairs, I'm not coming again!' Well, that was a terrible threat but the Beauforts, owners of Badminton, didn't have much money. The miniature run of carpet for the sole use of one Royal old lady was all they could afford.

*S*ir Peter Hall found himself in a bit of a bind when, emerging from the breakfast room at a Royal party for the 1977 Jubilee bearing three plates of scrambled eggs and with a cigar in his mouth, he bumped into the Duke of Edinburgh. How was he to speak? His difficulty was immediately resolved by a footman, who stepped up, removed the cigar from his mouth and stood by holding it until Sir Peter's conversation with the Duke was over. It is not known whether the attendant then put it back in the great man's mouth.

Family Rivalry – Who is the Loveliest of Them All?

*B*ig panic during rehearsals for George VI's Coronation – the orb, part of the near-sacred Coronation regalia, was nowhere to be found, until someone heard a giveaway rumbling from under a table. Princess Margaret, aged 6, had seized it and was rolling it around on the floor.

*I*n later life Princess Margaret was recalling younger and happier days when her father would be practising for Trooping the Colour at home and used to let her try on his bearskin. But her story came to a peculiar halt. Evidently there was something else of significance she had to say, something that almost couldn't be said. 'Sometimes . . .' she murmured, 'he let me put on the crown.'

At Windsor Castle Princess Margaret once flung open a door and shouted into the room where the Queen was sitting with some top person or other, 'Nobody would speak to you if you weren't the Queen!'

After a State Dinner at Windsor, there was a tour of the Castle, with the Queen as chief guide. The rest of the party was supposed to be listening respectfully. In a certain room, there was a pause and the Queen invited people to inspect various items that had been laid out. But Princess Margaret sat down on a sofa for a good old natter with Edna Healey about the latter's recent meeting with Group Captain Townsend. When the Queen moved off into another room, her sister stayed put. Can you imagine? An unfortunate attendant tried to drop a hint. 'Go away,' Princess Margaret snapped, 'I'm talking to Mrs Healey.'

One day Prince William was moaning about the forthcoming but surely distant burden of kingship. Quick as a flash, Prince Harry said, 'If you won't do it, then I will.'

There was an accident during a shooting lunch at Sandringham. A footman picked up a coffee pot and failed to notice that the gas burner it had been sitting over had somehow remained attached. It fell onto Princess Margaret whose napkin went up in flames. 'Oh, look, they're trying to set fire to Margo,' the Queen commented, with not a great deal of dismay.

The Queen Mother gave her eldest daughter not only her own first name but her own initials too. The Queen Mother was Elizabeth Angela Marguerite and the Queen is Elizabeth Alexandra Mary.

At her wedding, the Queen Mother left her tiny handbag in the carriage on arrival at the Abbey. When the Queen, as Princess Elizabeth, was married, she did exactly the same thing – either on purpose or by coincidence.

$\mathcal{A}$t Birkhall the Queen Mother had a huge ER cut out in a lawn and planted with French marigolds (not African, which she disliked). She said, 'One will do for me and the other for the Queen.' But which one? The R or the E?

$\mathcal{T}$he Queen Mother reeled in astonishment when, at lunch, the usually abstemious Queen asked for a second glass of wine. 'Are you sure, dear? You have got to reign all afternoon, you know.'

$\mathcal{B}$efore it was modernised in the 1970s, Sandringham was a terrible fire hazard. Frequent fire drills were necessary, during which members of the Royal Family would stand in one corner of the lawn, waiting to be counted, while other departments of the Household stood in other corners. On one occasion, Princess Margaret failed to appear. A harried maid appealed to the Queen Mother for help in getting her out of bed but the Princess's mother just said, 'Oh, well, she'll just have to burn, won't she?'

$\mathcal{W}$hen the Royal Family were touring South Africa together in 1947, Princess Elizabeth, as she then was, used her umbrella as a kind of cattle-prod if her mother, the Queen, was lingering too long in idle conversation. A quick jab in the ankles usually did the trick.

*P*rincess Margaret claimed that she drove the Lord Chamberlain up the wall by forever altering her funeral arrangements. At one time she had a whim to be buried at sea. But all the chopping and changing was worth it because what could have been more perfect than the ruse she finally came up with – to be cremated (never mind the indignity of Slough public crematorium) in order to be sufficiently reduced in size to fit snugly into the kingly tomb of her parents, George VI and Queen Elizabeth, leaving Lilibet to fend for herself elsewhere.

*A*t lunch at Windsor the Queen mentioned Gravadlax, at the time a novelty. 'It's pickled,' she explained. 'Raw salmon. Pickled. Quite extra-ordinary.' The other guests were intrigued, but Princess Margaret took exception. 'No, it isn't. It's smoked,' she insisted. The Queen explained patiently she had tried it herself, had made inquiries as to how it was made. 'No, it's smoked,' said Margaret. 'Otherwise it would go bad.' They carried on like this, good-naturedly, for some time until the Queen deftly changed the subject.*

*A*t a military dinner a drunken soldier staggered towards Princess Margaret, but before he could say anything disgraceful, the Colonel-in-Chief had the presence of mind to shout: 'Go away and sit down!' As they watched the man lurching back to his place, the Princess said, 'That's just what the Queen's always saying to her corgis but they don't take a blind bit of notice.'

*I*t's bad form to wear white to a wedding – competing with the bride. So why did the Queen choose a white wool coat for the Charles and Camilla Blessing Service in 2005? Especially suspicious when you think it's not a colour she

---

* In fact, Gravadlax is cured, but it certainly isn't smoked.

usually wears. And then, during the service, she upstaged the entire congregation by being the only one who could sing the whole of 'Immortal, invisible' without once referring to the service sheet.

*E*arly on in her affair with the Prince of Wales, Wallis Simpson began to get ideas above her station. Visiting Buckingham Palace at the Prince's insistence but, as far as everybody else was concerned, absolutely on sufferance, she looked out of the window and saw some of Queen Mary's favourite flower-beds. 'When I live here,' she remarked appreciatively, 'those will be tennis-courts.'

*T*here was much controversy over the 'improvements' Raine Spencer, Princess Diana's stepmother, made at Althorp. Particularly loathed was the ugly double-glazing, which was awkward to open and which the present Earl has largely removed. Visiting in the 1980s, Princess Diana complained about the lack of ventilation in her bedroom. But later in the visit she came up with a straightforward solution: she smashed the glass.

Who's in Charge?
The Struggle for Power

'I suppose he will want me to call him Tony,' was the Queen's way of greeting Blair's 1997 landslide victory.

Trying to be friendly, Cherie Blair allegedly said to Princess Anne, 'Do call me Cherie.' 'I think not actually,' was the Princess Royal's reply.

At Exeter Town Hall, not long after the foot and mouth crisis, the Queen encountered a member of the public who said, 'This Government doesn't care about the countryside.' 'I know,' the Queen replied. 'That's what I'm always telling Mr Blair when I see him every week.'

'Tell me a little more about what you've been doing?' the Queen asked a man whom she was about to invest with a CBE. 'I've been arguing with the Government,' he replied. Her Majesty seemed to be on his wavelength straightaway. 'Yes, governments do need arguing with sometimes,' she remarked.

'Who will be my conscience?' the Queen demanded after discovering that Tony Blair intended to abolish the post of Lord Chancellor. She was especially displeased that she had been kept in the dark on this occasion. 'Nobody tells me anything,' she complained to astonished onlookers in Edinburgh.

When, in the 1970s, the 1st Lord of the Admiralty was sent for, he found the Queen in a less than amenable frame of mind. Her *froideur* was occasioned by the public row that was going on about the cost of refitting the Royal Yacht *Britannia*. But the 1st Lord thought he had got the situation under control. All he needed to do was to explain in great detail what was the matter with *Britannia*. So he held forth at length about turbines and bulkheads and the rest of it. He

26

came to the end of his oration. But the Queen
was unthawed. 'Who pays?' she inquired thinly.
The 1st Lord cheered up a bit. Oh, if that was
all she was worried about ... 'The Government
pays,' he said breezily. But still the Queen glared
at him. 'I see,' she said eventually. 'You pay and
I get the blame.'

On arrival at Balmoral for the annual visit of his
father, the Prime Minister, little Leo Blair had
a present ready for his hosts. It was a loyal recital
of the first verse of the National Anthem. As
far as the Queen and the Duke of Edinburgh
were concerned, this more than made up for the
possible Republican tendencies of his mother,
Cherie. The visit got off to a flying start. The Duke
of Edinburgh set to work at once teaching the
boy the second verse – it's not known whether
it was the version which goes: 'O Lord our God
above/Scatter her enemies/And make them fall'.

*D*uring one of the Queen's absences abroad, the Queen Mother, as Counsellor of State, conducted a meeting of the Privy Council at Clarence House. Lord St John of Fawsley was present. Afterwards she said, 'You must all be so tired after your official duties. Would you care to stay for a gin and tonic?' But the meeting had lasted only a few minutes.

*W*hile it may not be true that, during her audiences with Mrs Thatcher, the Queen felt as though she were being addressed as if at a public meeting, she did go about asking rather strange questions about her Prime Minister. 'Is Mrs Thatcher religious?' she inquired of Archbishop Runcie. And what about this, asked of Lord Carrington, who has never disclosed his reply: '*Will Mrs Thatcher change?*'

*I*n the 1960s, Richard Crossman, at that time a member of the Government, refused to attend the State Opening of Parliament, claiming that he had no morning suit. The Queen found this provoking. She said that she too disliked official ceremonies but could hardly offer that or any other excuse to get out of them.

*T*ony Blair's 1970s let-it-all-hang-out side was on display when, on TV, he entered the Queen's sitting room for his weekly audience, and flung himself into a chair *while the Queen remained standing*.

'*A*re you still waving your stick around?' the Queen asked Edward Heath, some time after he had ceased to be Prime Minister. She referred to his sideline in conducting orchestras.

*G*eorge Brown, Labour Chancellor in the 1960s, a raffish figure often the worse for wear, always addressed the Queen as 'My dear'.

*A*t a party in London for the Commonwealth Conference, conversation in the Queen's little group appeared to be rumbling along as usual until suddenly Her Majesty was to be heard shrieking 'Oh, but you're completely dispensable' and all but poking a somewhat huffy Edward Heath, to whom she referred, in the ribs.

In his glory days of power, Edward Heath was deeply miffed that his car was held up in Parliament Square for 20 minutes in order to allow the cavalcade of the Queen Mother to pass by.

'That's where the trouble started,' said George VI to Anthony Blunt as they drove past Runnymede.

'Don't make me laugh when Dennis does his bow,' the Queen murmured to an equerry as the Thatchers made their way across the carpet.

In the 1960s, Tony Benn, an enthusiastic young Republican, became Postmaster General and conceived a passion to get the Queen's head removed from the stamps. Courtiers at Buckingham Palace were, needless to say, far from encouraging. But Benn thought if he could only speak to the main person, it might be a different story. So an audience with the Queen was arranged and, sure enough, she said she had no view one way or the other about her head on the stamps. Benn went away in triumph, only to find thickets of bureaucratic obfuscation springing up all around him. Courtiers continued to suggest that, on the whole, headless stamps were not on. The affair dragged on interminably. The Prime Minister was rather busy with other, more important, matters. In the end Benn started to wonder if he wasn't beginning to look a little foolish, banging on about the stamps. He decided to forget about them. Shortly afterwards, he stepped down as Postmaster General and took another Cabinet post. On going to kiss hands, the Queen said, 'I'm sure you'll miss your stamps.'

*A*t a Privy Council meeting in the 1960s, the counsellors, of whom on this occasion there were quite a number, found themselves on their knees in the Royal presence, *on the wrong side of the room*. Rather than standing up and moving to the right side in the normal manner, they plainly thought it would be less conspicuous and more respectful if they were to shuffle across, still prone. So this is

what they did. In the process, someone collided with a table and the Queen had to stoop to pick up a dislodged book. By the time they'd all got to where they were supposed to be, the look on the Queen's face suggested that they would be headless by tea-time. When the sadly bungled ceremony was over, the Clerk of the Council went back into the room to apologise. 'Oh, don't worry,' the Queen said. 'I was just trying not to laugh.'

Sometimes being Prime Minister just isn't enough if you really want to get things done. In 1965 Ian Smith, the renegade leader of Rhodesia, came to London for Churchill's funeral and Harold Wilson saw an opportunity to carry on negotiations over the future of that country informally. He asked the Queen to invite him to her reception for world leaders, even though he wasn't representing a sovereign Government. But the wretched man had the cheek not to turn up. The reception was in progress and Wilson was downcast. 'Leave it to me,' said the Queen. She despatched her equerry, who found Smith tucking into his lunch at the Hyde Park Hotel. All sense of having got one over deserted him at the sight of the Royal emissary. He'd never received the invitation, he said. Yes, of course, he'd come at once.

They're Really Quite Normal

A few years ago Sir Roy Strong went to the Queen's party at Buckingham Palace for people in the Arts. A few days later he happened to see the Queen again, so he took the opportunity to thank her. 'Oh,' she replied, 'did you like it?' 'Yes,' he said. 'Everyone was there I can't usually get on the telephone.' 'I never knew who was there,' the Queen remarked. 'I'd forgotten to put my specs on.'

*I*n 1972, Sir Hardy Amies clubbed together with Freddie Fox and gave the Queen a chinchilla hat for Christmas. Not really her kind of thing, you'd have thought – more Julie Christie in *Doctor Zhivago* than HM. But she told Sir Hardy that, although as a rule she did not accept such expensive presents, on this occasion the glamorous item had completely overwhelmed her idea of what was sensible.

*T*he Queen was sitting for her portrait at Buckingham Palace when she noticed a ladder in her stockings. Since, when being painted, she becomes talkative, this alarming detail came spilling out. The artist asked if she would like to end the sitting early. No thank you, the Queen said. 'I'll just have time to change before the next thing.' The session over, the Monarch charged out of the room and was seen by the dumbfounded painter running at full pelt down the corridor.

*A*t the end of a sitting the artist Terence Cuneo asked the Queen to sign a print of his painting of the Coronation. Oh woe! His pen wouldn't work. 'I think I'd better fetch mine,' said the Queen. Twenty minutes later, having been to the other end of the Palace, she returned.

*I*n the 1960s, the Queen tried to resist the dictates of fashion but in the end even she had to give in to shorter skirts. In 1971 she told Sir Hardy Amies that she was pleased with her new clothes – despite the new hemlines.

'*R*eady, girls!' the Queen exhorted over her shoulder to her maids-of-honour as her procession was about to enter Westminster Abbey on the occasion of her Coronation.

*D*uring the War, Sir Owen Morshead, the Royal Librarian, arranged a little treat for the two Princesses and their governess. He took them down into the vaults of the Castle. There they came across what appeared to be some battered old hatboxes stuffed with newspaper. On closer inspection, they turned out to contain the Crown Jewels. This was their wartime hiding place.

*I*t's such an awful *faux pas* to get someone's military rank wrong (especially if you demote them). So you can imagine Jilly Cooper's mortification when she discovered that in the acknowledgements of her brilliant jodhpur ripper, *Riders*, she'd put *Captain* Andrew Parker Bowles when it should have been Colonel. This was no way to repay him for the help he'd given her on equestrian matters while she was writing the book. Most of all she dreaded the response of his wife, Camilla, for it is usually the military wives who take the greater umbrage in these situations. But, when she met her for the first time, Mrs Parker Bowles thought it was extremely funny. 'Take him down a peg!' she said without a trace of malice.

*F*or many years, the Duchess of Cornwall holidayed on Corfu, where she used to whiz about on a moped.

*D*on't bother e-mailing Prince William. He never checks his inbox.

*W*hen she came to lunch with him, Cecil Beaton caught the Queen Mother hesitating over the cutlery and glancing at the other guests to see which knife and fork *they* were using.

*O*ne time the Queen was late for an engagement because she was so entranced by the display of Christmas crackers at Harrods.

*I*t was awful on board *Britannia* as she sailed through a storm past the Western Isles. The next morning the Queen remarked, 'I was lying there and I was thinking – there's nothing for it . . . I'll have to abdicate.'

*T*here is only one person the Queen is truly in awe of and that's the Duke of Edinburgh. Once, the Duke was driving at high speed and the Queen, in the front passenger seat, was drawing breath conspicuously in the manner of nervous passengers. 'If you carry on doing that, I'm going to stop the car and put you out,' the Duke said. When they reached their destination, Lord Mountbatten, who had been in the back seat, asked the Queen why she hadn't put up more resistance. 'You heard what he said,' was her simple response.

*I*n all weathers, the Queen likes a rug over her knees when driving. Possibly her cars have no heating. Often, while her car is stopped outside a place she is visiting, her chauffeur will be seen getting out, opening the back door and picking up the rug which the untidy Queen has thrown on the floor. He then folds it up nicely for when she comes back.

*S*ome members of the Royal Household work in buildings quite remote from any of the palaces. They see the Queen maybe twice a year at most and then not to speak to. So, you can imagine the surprise of one such member of staff who was gazing out of his window in an idle moment one morning. Suddenly a woman was waving to him from a passing car. He took quite a few seconds to realise it was the Queen. *She*, of course, forgets no one.

*I*n 2000, the Queen thought she'd cracked the secret of a good family Christmas. Get a wide age range, she told a friend. In her case, it went from the Queen Mother, then 99, to two babies. She enjoys having the house full, but she likes to be quiet afterwards. In 1979, she had told the same friend that it was very peaceful being snowed in at Sandringham with just the Duke of Edinburgh and a grandson for company.

*W*hen, owing to a secretarial error, Annigoni failed to turn up for a sitting, he feared the worst. But the Queen said she'd had an hour off, she could do exactly what she liked and 'nobody knew anything about it'. She was thrilled.

*T*he Queen is subject to noise nuisance at Buckingham Palace. In her bedroom she can hear traffic roaring up and down Constitution Hill, and then there are the sirens. 'Some days we've counted twenty or more,' she once remarked.

*N*o guarantee of night-time peace and quiet in other Royal residences, either. At Sandringham servants having a 'nightcap' kept Princess Diana awake. She found that earplugs were the only solution.

*P*eople who find it difficult to manage their in-trays will be encouraged to know that the Queen shares their problem – only perhaps with rather more excuse. In 1962, she wrote to apologise to Sir Hardy Amies, explaining that she had done what she often did – put his letter in her red box where it had got covered by a whole lot of other things and then, she was sorry to say, forgotten about! She had found it again only after two months and was terribly sorry to be so late in replying.

*A*t a wedding at St James's Palace something very conspiratorial, involving a great deal of giggling, was going on between the Queen and Penelope Keith.

The Queen Mother often surprised pedestrians by winding down her window, should her car be stopped in traffic, and addressing them. On one occasion someone sneezed and was amazed to find that the person saying 'Bless you' was the bejewelled and befeathered Queen Mother. Another time a young man had his arm in plaster and was sitting disconsolately on a bench beside the road. 'Oh, dear, what has happened?' a voice said. It was the Queen Mother in sweet-pea prints, speaking from the back of her car. 'I fell off my bike,' the person replied in a very small voice. 'Oh, dear. It's always the bike, isn't it?' said Her Majesty consolingly before moving off.

It seemed odd that the Queen Mother, when she visited Rhodesia and Nyasaland in 1960, preferred to be alone on long car drives. Eventually spies found out that, as soon as her car was clear of the crowds, she would kick off her shoes, put her feet up and tuck in to a nice bag of toffees which she kept in her handbag.

Even Royalty can be overawed in the presence of screen legends. Meeting Lauren Bacall, Prince Charles couldn't think of anything to say. 'I so enjoyed your black-and-white films,' he spluttered eventually. 'I'm not that old, Prince,' the star growled.

*I*n the late 1960s, people in the receiving line at the première of *Cyrano de Bergerac* at the Old Vic thought that Princess Margaret was looking especially fine with her hair swept up high off her forehead. It was only when she had passed by and they could see the back view that they realised something was wrong. What were all these funny little tufts of hair bunched up with rubber bands? This didn't seem to be a continuation of the grand scheme suggested by the front view. It was an endearing sight but surely not intended. No indeed. Eventually someone got it. There was supposed to be a hairpiece (for this was the era of the hairpiece) at the back, but, for some reason, it was missing. The Princess was quietly steered into a side-room and kept there until the adornment could be fetched from Kensington Palace. She explained that she had had to leave the house in a rush.

*I*n 1958, the Queen Mother's aircraft broke down at Mauritius and she was held up for three days.

When eventually she got back to London, she was wearing a tweed coat *with white shoes* – even Royalty can only pack so much.

*P*rincess Margaret went for Sunday lunch at the home of her friend the theatre designer Carl Toms. She turned out to be a great help in the kitchen, and sorted out the sink, which was cluttered up with dirty pots and pans, in no time.

*D*uring the War, Nicky Haslam recalls, the Queen Mother, then Queen, visited bombed-out Clapham. 'Where do you live, little boy?' she inquired of a small child. 'Opposite Arding and 'obbs,' was the squeaky answer. 'How strange,' said the Queen. 'I live opposite Gorringe.' She always insisted on referring to her neighbourhood department store (now defunct) as 'Gorringe', not 'Gorringes' like everybody else.

$\mathcal{A}$ painting by Prince William was exhibited at Eton to great acclaim. Comparisons were made with Howard Hodgkin and Mark Rothko. Until, that is, the Prince patiently explained that it was a picture of a house – gone wrong.

$\mathcal{P}$rince William doesn't miss a promotional opportunity. Meeting John Savident, who plays the butcher in *Coronation Street*, he asked why he didn't have organic bacon in his shop. 'Duchy of Cornwall's good, you know.'

$\mathcal{B}$ored at Balmoral during the first summer of her marriage, Princess Diana and a friend sought some diversion. How about shopping in Ballater? So they trudged off down the drive and caught the bus into town. Frightful ructions in the security department when it was discovered that they were missing.

$\mathcal{T}$hinking a policeman was looking a little wan, the Queen Mother, about to get into her car, opened her handbag and produced a piece of barley sugar. 'That'll keep you going!' she said.

*I*n the winter of 1981 the Queen was returning by Land Rover from a visit to her daughter, Princess Anne, at Gatcombe Park when heavy snow began to fall. She was forced to seek shelter at the Cross Hands Hotel, Sodbury, at that time something of a two-star, chicken-in-a-basket and coleslaw type of establishment. She sat in a twin-bedded room with a brown nylon carpet and lemon-yellow candlewick bedspreads, watching television. The manager showed her the menu, which also featured quiche, chicken Kiev (a favourite at Buckingham Palace) and Black Forest gateau. She asked for only a cup of tea. She remained in the room for seven hours.

*T*he Queen generates a lot of static electricity. This means she can't wear silk, crêpe de chine or chiffon next to the skin. They would cling. Anyone might be a 'clinger', as they are known in the trade. It isn't a condition arising from the Queen's unique position in life.

*O*n the other hand the Queen isn't a 'wriggler'. She can stand still while her couturiers and their assistants swirl about her.

*T*he Queen Mother and Norman Hartnell liked to listen to the *Jimmy Young Show* during fittings. The Recipe of the Day was a particular highlight.

'*W*e must struggle on as best we can.' Thus one working woman to another – the Queen Mother, over 90, bucking up her lady-in-waiting, Lady Hambledon, much the same age.

'*I*t's for my nanny,' Prince Harry thoughtfully explained to a somewhat wide-eyed assistant at Selfridges as she popped his purchase into a bag. It was a marabou-trimmed thong.

Home Life

'Welcome to the peace of my own home,' the Queen began one of her early Christmas broadcasts on TV, which, in those days, were always live. In fact the electricians had drilled a hole through the wall for a cable and the peace of her own home was rather ruined by a howling draft. The Queen nearly froze in her thin satin frock.

On New Year's Day, Princess Margaret always waltzed alone in her bedroom as the New Year's Day concert was being relayed from Vienna on the radio.

When the Queen commissioned Reynolds Stone (he designed the £5 and £10 notes) to do an engraving for her private writing paper, she said, 'I want a view of my bedroom. Not *from* my bedroom, but of it – from outside on the lawn.' An odd choice.

Here is an interesting insight into Royal eating habits. One day it was asparagus for lunch. The Queen began to eat hers with her fingers as soon as it was put before her. Next to her, an officer, who would be the last to be served, watched anxiously, wondering how he would manage this awkward food. It was quite a prolonged agony of waiting. By the time he got his, the Queen had finished hers. She said encouragingly, 'Now it's my turn to watch you make a pig of yourself.'

Prince Charles did manage to persuade the Queen Mother to invite Mrs Parker Bowles to lunch. It wasn't really a success. The Queen Mother was a friend of Andrew Parker Bowles and anyway not game for being brought up to date *vis-à-vis* modern relationships. At one point Camilla put her elbows on the table. The Queen Mother was very concerned. 'Are you feeling quite well, dear?' she inquired.

Astonishing goings-on at the Castle of Mey in the 1990s. The young equerries got tremendously overexcited, rushing about in the night hiding one another's sheets and pouring bottles of disinfectant over each other. They must have thought they were back at school. In the morning the Queen Mother remarked to one of her long-serving retainers, 'Do you know, there was someone in my bedroom last night brandishing a soda siphon?' She didn't seem that bothered.

A senior member of the Queen Mother's household later confirmed that the equerries weren't drunk. 'It was just high spirits. There was never a dull minute when you were with the Queen Mother.'

So it would seem.

A certain amount of horror spread among the nudists on Holkham beach when the Duke of Edinburgh strode past with his carriage-driving partner, Lady Romsey. But they needn't have worried. He raised his hat and said, 'Good morning' in the most neighbourly way.

We've all heard about the Tupperware boxes on the Queen's breakfast table, but now there's more news of grim conditions at Buckingham Palace. Her Majesty was once looking through a pile of thank-you letters for a State dinner. 'They all mention the food. I can't think why. I didn't cook it.' Then she paused meaningfully. 'Besides, we all know what the food's like here.'

Another time, the chef was upset because the main course of a banquet had been served none too hot. The Queen cheered him up. 'People don't come here for the food, hot or cold. They come here to eat off gold plate.'

When he was first married, the Duke of Edinburgh was disconcerted to find his wife's nursery maid from her childhood, Bobo MacDonald, still doggedly at her station in the bathroom. She would run her mistress's bath, then stay on, parked comfortably at one end, for a chat. In these circumstances, the Duke could hardly come in. Some thought that was the plan.

In 1974, Bobo MacDonald had a nasty accident and broke her collarbone and four ribs. The Queen had to set off on a tour of the South Seas without her. She wrote to Sir Hardy Amies: 'I really will have to think out clothes for myself this time!'

Dining alone at Buckingham Palace, the Queen was presented with something that might once have been a piece of fish. She banged it with the back of her fork. Turning to Paul Burrell (for it was he), she inquired, 'What do you suggest I do with this?' Her footman offered to return to the kitchen and fetch something else. 'No,' said the Queen, 'don't take it back. I don't want anyone to get into trouble.' She had a miserable dinner of vegetables and salad.

Perhaps the Queen really would prefer to do her own cooking. She knows a surprising amount about it. Her correspondence with other Heads of State veers alarmingly from solemn consideration of weighty matters to jolly chat about children's toys, horses and *recipes*. In 1959 she sent General Eisenhower, who was then US President, her recipe for drop scones, he having expressed an

interest. She explained helpfully how to adjust
the quantities for a number less than 16 and said
that she always whisked the mixture thoroughly
and didn't let it stand around before cooking.
The President replied that he hadn't known what
'caster' sugar was and had had to ring up the
British Embassy.

Guests at a little pre-theatre supper at Buckingham Palace in the 1960s were surprised to find the
Queen struggling alone, not a servant in sight. To
cap it all, there was no mustard. 'If I ring the bell,'
she explained, 'no one will come for at least half an
hour.' The only hope seemed to be to go to the
door and shout down the corridor – which is what
she did.

The Queen has the newspaper propped up on the mantelpiece during fittings. When not reading, she might nibble on a Mars bar.

The Sandringham staff party one year was fancy dress. The Queen Mother came as Stalin.

As a new boy at Buckingham Palace in 1951, the Duke of Edinburgh was mystified – not to say irritated – by the unfailing appearance, every evening, of a new bottle of whisky in the Queen's bedroom. What was it doing there? Neither he nor the Queen had asked for it. He made inquiries but got nowhere. Apparently it was just the done thing for whisky to be placed in the Sovereign's bedroom at night. Well, that wasn't good enough for the Duke. He was determined to burrow further into the matter. In the end he had to open up the archives. It turned out that, one day 80 or so years earlier, Queen Victoria had had a cold and asked for Scotch. Receiving no instructions to the contrary, the servants had continued to put the bottle in the bedroom ever since.

Kenneth Clark recalled spending a jolly evening with the Queen, later Queen Mother, in the lodge-keeper's room at Windsor tasting country wines.

John Julius Norwich reports on the unusual effect of alcohol on the Queen Mother. Lunching annually at All Souls College, Oxford, she would have a minimum of two gin and Dubonnets beforehand and plenty of wine during. But the result was not a slowing down but a speeding up. Afterwards, she absolutely pounded, in a dead straight line, across three quads to her car, talking all the way.

Queen Mary always insisted that her outfit had two concealed pockets – one for her hanky and the other for a secret supply of biscuits.

Queen Mary often wrote to Sir Owen Morshead, the Royal Librarian, from Badminton during the War, concerned as to the whereabouts of certain Royal possessions. What had happened to a table runner embroidered by Princess Beatrice or a pair of Chinese slippers that had belonged to the Empress Frederick? Would he please look in the third drawer down of the chest of drawers in such and such a room along such and such a corridor of the Castle? Sure enough, there they were.

The Queen Mother was not always as keen on a drop as has been suggested. Picnicking on a wild Scottish moor, she asked a friend to pour her gin and Dubonnet. She took one sip, pronounced it 'far too strong' and tipped it into the heather.

Ham sandwiches were an enduring bedtime feature throughout the Queen Mother's life. On a State Visit to Canada in 1937 with George VI, instructions were issued that ham sandwiches were always to be available in the Royal bedroom, no matter how substantial the preceding dinner or

banquet had been. In later life the Queen Mother ordered 250 hams a year from Peasenhall in Suffolk. For greater comfort, she preferred to eat the sandwiches once she was actually in bed.

*T*he Queen Mother was relieved to get back to Birkhall in time for tea after the funeral of Diana, Princess of Wales and the other rather trying events of that week. 'Ah tea!' she said, as soon as she was through the front door, taking comfort in the lavish array of scones, cakes and shortbread.

*I*t might seem rather reckless to get into a debate about the Monarchy when your hostess is Princess Margaret, but that is what happened to Lord St John of Fawsley. He, of course, was pro, but the person he was talking to really did take his life in his hands when, *with Princess Margaret standing hard by*, he remarked loudly, 'Oh, don't listen to him. He's just a professional Royal supporter.' But all the Princess said was, 'Yes, and that is a very good profession to belong to.' It was a lucky escape.

Don't I Get No Respect?

*I*n the 1920s, the British Ambassadress in Paris saw somebody standing about, apparently at a loose end. 'Young man,' she said, 'would you open that window?' She had failed to recognise the Duke of York, later George VI, who was supposed to be the Guest of Honour. Later, feeling the strain of the Royal visit, she inquired of her private secretary, 'Am I doing all right, Bill?' Only it wasn't Bill. It was the Duke of York again.

*H*enry Marten, vice-Provost of Eton, was drafted in to teach Princess Elizabeth history. Frequently, unable or unwilling to adapt to his new audience, he addressed her as 'Gentlemen'.

*D*uring the 1947 Royal Tour of South Africa, the Royal train arrived at George, a town in the southern Cape. The organisers had gone to a great deal of trouble but they had made one little mistake. A huge banner had been stretched across the processional route, proclaiming 'Welcome to George'. As the Queen Mother, then Queen, drove under it, she sighed wistfully to her companion, 'They seem to have forgotten about *me*.'

*T*he Queen Mother liked to visit Fortnum and Mason every Christmas to see the display of crackers. One year she found the exhibition not only drastically reduced in scale but shoved away under the stairs. She was most put out.

*A*s the Queen Mother's car was going from London to Windsor, her policeman, sitting in the front, was sound asleep. When the car stopped suddenly he woke up. His first thought was his duty. They had arrived, so he must leap out and open the back door for Her Majesty. Only then did things begin to appear a little less than straight-forward. 'Where are we?' she said, apparently confused. On closer inspection of the surroundings the policeman was able to establish that they were in fact in the Cromwell Road Extension. 'Perhaps we'll go a little further today,' the Queen Mother suggested.

$\mathcal{A}$ member of the public, wandering on the vast, wild beach at Holkham in Norfolk, noticed a lady struggling out of her bathing suit and another lady standing nearby. Coming closer, he recognised Lady Glenconner, once lady-in-waiting to Princess Margaret. Since in Norfolk anyone met by royalty is treated as a neighbour rather than a commoner, this lady said, 'Do you know Mrs Parker Bowles?', who was still in some turmoil with her bathing suit. 'Oh,' said the man, taken by surprise, 'you look a lot better than in your photographs, I must say.' Clinging on to her towel, Camilla wasn't a bit put out. 'How kind of you,' she said. 'Thank you very much.'

$\mathcal{O}$nce, in the 1970s, rushing back from the swimming pool at Buckingham Palace, the Prince of Wales was leapt upon by a man bearing an enormous bundle of laundry. 'You press!' this person commanded, forcing the clothes into the Prince's arms. It turned out that the staff of the President of Zaire, whose State Visit was in progress, were less clued up than they might have been.

'*W*hat happened after I left?' is a favourite question of the Prince of Wales if he has been to a party. Relieved of his presence, people might be just a little less ... constrained, shall we say? He knows this.

*I*n 1947, two young women sharing lodgings were making toast when they heard the news of Princess Elizabeth's engagement on the wireless. They were so excited they forgot the toast and it got burnt. To commemorate the event, they sent the results to Buckingham Palace. By the time the burnt toast arrived it had become rather unpleasant.

*I*n the 1960s, the Queen sometimes drove around London in a Mini. When she drew up at Micky Sekers's fabric shop, she told the lady-in-waiting to watch out for the parking attendants. 'They're hot round here,' was her way of putting it.

The Queen had student trouble at Buckingham Palace when a drunken Oxford undergraduate gatecrashed Prince Charles's birthday party in the 1960s. The Queen said she had seen him herself. 'He was so drunk he was only able to utter a few incivilities.' Can you imagine? But she didn't want him sent down.

At Clarence House on hot days, it seemed enchanting to lunch in a shady bower created by plane trees. There were two '*salles vertes*', one the '*salon*' with armchairs and the other the '*salle à manger*' with mahogany table and every accoutrement. But there was another reason for being under or more accurately *inside* the trees. The Queen Mother suffered from nosy neighbours, in this case people peering at her out of the windows of Lancaster House, next door.

The Queen Mother had an encounter with a mynah bird at the Sandringham Flower Show one year. The bird inquired, 'Can your mother skin a rabbit?' 'I'm really not sure,' was the reply. 'Well, clear off then!'

*P*resident Roosevelt's mother knew just what was needed for the King and Queen's visit to her home in 1939 – a new lavatory seat. But when the plumber submitted his bill after the Royal visit, Mrs Roosevelt was outraged at the expense and refused to pay. The plumber said, 'Well, I'll have that seat back then.' The cheeky devil then made a display of it in his shop window. The caption read: 'The King and Queen sat here.'

*T*he Queen Mother often visited her racing manager, Peter Cazalet, quite unaccompanied. Once she arrived early and wandered into the stables to find the 12-year-old son of the house messing around with a terrible old Ford Popular. To her astonishment he offered her a lift in this appalling machine. Setting aside any misgivings she might have had, she got in and soon found herself launched on the sort of drive a 12-year-old boy with a clapped-out vehicle and extensive grounds at his disposal *would* enjoy. Every pot-hole, sharp bend, slippery patch and puddle was sought out and made the most of. Actually reaching their destination was given the lowest conceivable priority. The Queen Mother was thrilled to bits.

*O*pponents of the Queen Mother's at Racing Demon often became depressed. There was just no beating her. 'I'm suwwounded by howwible, howwible Queens,' one exasperated player cried out.

*B*arbara Cartland, step-grandmother of Diana Spencer, announced that she was far too old to attend the Royal Wedding of 1981. In fact, she had not been invited. All the same, some people put their thinking caps on. If B. Cartland was too old at 79, where did that leave the Queen Mother, who was almost 81 at the time?

*T*he Duke of Edinburgh had no choice but to challenge an officer before dinner about his appearance. 'What's this ordinary white shirt in aid of? You're supposed to be wearing a dress shirt, aren't you?' 'I only wear that on special occasions,' the officer replied.

*I*t is rarely mentioned that the Queen Mother, when she was Queen, also had an intruder in her bedroom at Buckingham Palace, although not, apparently, when she was actually asleep. During the War a deserter flung himself on the floor and gripped the Queen by her ankles. He had lost all his family in an air raid. As her daughter was to do 40 years later, Her Majesty coaxed the man into a calmer mood before summoning help.

*A*n officer was doing his rounds at Windsor, checking up on his men, when a footman appeared and announced that the Queen was suggesting tea. This was a delightful prospect, not, of course to be refused. It was a hot day, and Her Majesty was most insistent her guest should remove his greatcoat ... Oh, dear. Unforeseen drawback to undreamed-of Royal intimacy. This officer, as was customary among his peers, had not bothered to put on his tunic under his coat, as he was supposed to do. Underneath, he was just wearing a vest. So, several times, he had to refuse his Sovereign's invitation to make himself comfortable, all the time getting hotter and hotter, both literally and metaphorically. Eventually inspiration struck. He told the Queen he had been suffering from 'flu. Would it be all right if he kept his coat on?

A game of sardines was in progress at Sandringham. One guest was hiding under a table and became aware of another presence in the darkness. 'Who is it?' he whispered. 'Elizabeth,' was the reply. He then had to remain motionless and silent under the table with the Queen for the next twenty minutes.

*T*he Duke of Edinburgh, walking near Balmoral, was annoyed to find a youth in his path. He gave him quite a ticking off. 'You can't just wander about anywhere, you know. Now, just what do you think you're doing?' 'But you don't understand,' said the boy, 'I'm doing my Duke of Edinburgh Award.' There wasn't really any answer to that.

$\mathcal{A}$n Eton boy was once late back from a dinner engagement at Windsor Castle. But he had a chit from King George VI to explain. You'd have thought it would have been good enough. But H. K. Marsden, a famously bad-tempered master, exploded, 'The chap hasn't even bothered to date it,' and threw the note away.

$\mathcal{T}$he portrait painter Pietro Annigoni complained to the Duchess of Devonshire that the Queen talked too much during her sittings. At the next session, he was most disturbed to find Her Majesty completely silent. It was true that the Duchess had said, 'I'll tell her so,' but he hadn't imagined that she *actually would*.

$\mathcal{A}$t premières Princess Margaret was an exceptionally enthusiastic social kisser. Sometimes those not paying enough attention found themselves being kissed before they'd quite realised who it was.

$\mathcal{R}$ivalry between the Queen and Elizabeth Taylor goes back some way. In 1977, the film star got the upper hand at the British Embassy in Washington, when, by great good fortune, her gown tore in the queue and the whole business of getting it repaired and her subsequent late entry into the party meant that she got all the TV coverage while Her Majesty was overlooked. Then, in 2000, Elizabeth Taylor was to be invested with a DBE at Buckingham Palace. But she had numerous questions: could the quarantine rules be waived so she could take her dog with her to Britain? Could she bring her own security guards? Even, it was said, could she be late? How much flexibility was there? Whatever the case, she was on time, she didn't bring her own heavies and the dog stayed at home.

*P*rince William was stopped in the street in St Andrews by a woman who asked him the best place to buy underwear. Apparently she hadn't recognised him. But she must have been up to something, waylaying a nice young man and

asking suggestive questions, don't you think? The Prince was superbly nonchalant in his reply by the way.

*A*n unfortunate culture clash occurred when a Geordie councillor was invited to tea at Buckingham Palace. The Queen inquired, 'Would you like cake or meringue?' 'No, y'er not wrang, Your Majesty,' the councillor replied. 'I'll have the cake.'

*V*isiting the theatre informally in the 1960s, the Queen and her party sat in the stalls. A drunk man sitting two rows behind took pleasure in flicking paper pellets at them to see if they would lodge in the ladies' hair. One lady felt her hair becoming quite laden but the Queen, apparently, noticed nothing.

*I*n a busy commuter train at the height of the Abdication Crisis in 1936, silence reigned as passengers pored in horror over the newspapers. Nobody knew what to think. Until, that is, a kindly builder, complete with tool kit, spoke up: 'It's Queen Mary I feel sorry for. Poor old cow.'

*I*n later life Queen Mary's wave from her Daimler became so regular that it was said that she was in fact asleep and being worked off the back axle.

*S*ir Michael Duff specialised in dressing up as Queen Mary, driving round London in a car identical to her own and waving to passers-by, who assumed it was the real thing. On one occasion, he drew up at a grand party. Guests came rushing out. 'You can't come in!' they screamed. 'She's already here.'

*Q*ueen Mary's ladies-in-waiting all had funny names. There was Lizzie Motion and Puss Milnes-Gaskell. Another, Lady Juliet Duff, was once visited by Queen Mary in her block of flats. Lady Juliet's son, Sir Michael Duff (the same one who had a sideline in dressing up as Her Majesty) was waiting by the old-fashioned lift, which was like a cage you could see into, to greet the Royal visitor. He heard gates slamming below, then the clunking of machinery, followed shortly by the heaving into view of Queen Mary's toque, then her stern unmoving face with its swaying earrings, the substantial bosom, and of course the furled umbrella, planted before her. But what was this? Why were Queen Mary's shoes now at eye level? And then disappearing altogether in continued ascent? The lift came to rest somewhere above. There was more clunking and whirring of machinery, but never the sound of a human voice. Sir Michael braced himself once again to receive Her Majesty. Soon the Royal feet, and the umbrella tip re-appeared. But, would you believe it, as before, the entire motionless Royal ensemble slid silently by and Sir Michael found himself gazing at the top of Queen Mary's toque once again as she missed her stop for the second time. Only on the third attempt did she dock.

*W*hile she was sitting for Annigoni at Clarence House, the Queen Mother would sometimes be spotted by passers-by in the street. Then a crowd would form and Her Majesty would have to hide. Queen Victoria suffered in a similar way when the

North Terrace at Windsor was open to the public. She would find nosy parkers with their faces pressed up to the window while she was trying to have a nice sit-down after lunch.

Going About My Business

The Queen always refers to her official monarchical activities as 'going about my business'.

At the Queen's Coronation there was only one little hitch. The carpet had been put down with the pile in the wrong direction. This meant the Queen's heavy embroidered dress wouldn't slide along nicely. In fact, to begin with she couldn't move at all. She had to signal to the Archbishop of Canterbury, 'Get me going.' He gave her a discreet shove.

The Queen's first visit to Trinity College, Oxford, turned out to be a wild affair. At lunch the Lord Lieutenant, Lord Macclesfield, keeled over in a faint. Inspired by her husband's example, his wife followed suit. Then, at the end of his speech, Harold Macmillan, the Chancellor of the University, nearly sat down on the floor because his chair had been removed. Upon leaving the Queen said, 'We've had a wonderful lunch. Bodies all over the place.'

*I*n South Africa the Queen Mother was delighted with the gracious farewell offered by the organiser of an exhibition she had visited. Why, he was even walking along beside her car as it moved off. What nice manners! Then, as the car left the crowds behind and began to move a little faster, there he still was, but trotting and looking rather hot. When the car really began to gather speed, and the man, now sprinting, started to turn a nasty colour, the Queen Mother wondered if this wasn't taking loyalty too far. Fortunately at exactly that moment she saw what the problem was. She ordered the car to stop at once. The man could then release his tie, which had been trapped in the door.

*I*n Papua New Guinea Prince Charles was to conduct an investiture. But with the ladies almost topless, where were the medals to be pinned? His valet came up with an ingenious solution – necklaces made of safety pins. Then the medals could be hung round their necks.

On a Royal visit to St Albans Abbey in January 2006, the Duchess of Cornwall spied a ladder in a corner and attempted to make an unscheduled ascent. 'Not in those shoes,' her lady-in-waiting said firmly, bringing the runaway Duchess back into line.

In an official visit to an island in the South Seas in the 1970s, Prince Charles was conveyed in the only car in the place – a Morris Minor held together by string. Other dignitaries were mounted on bicycles.

The informality of the Duchess of Cornwall on engagements will take some getting used to. Visiting the Unicorn Theatre, Southwark in March 2006, she sat on a bench with the rest of the audience to watch the performance. This was too much for the person sitting next to her, Roisin Seiffert, aged 9, who was overcome with giggles.

*D*uring the War, Queen Mary drove over to Oxford from Badminton for an engagement. Owing to petrol shortages, she had no support vehicle. The inevitable happened and her un-accompanied Daimler broke down. Her Majesty was stranded. Her detective flagged down a passing van but its back-seat was occupied by onions. So Queen Mary had to sit in the minion's position in the front while her lady-in-waiting was perched on top of the onions. Thus they proceeded to Oxford.

*V*isiting the bombed-out East End during the War, the Queen Mother, then Queen, helped a disabled mother to change her baby.

*I*n Canada the Duke of Edinburgh was intro-duced to the writer Carol Shields. 'What do you write about?' he inquired. 'I write about women and their problems.' The Duke's eyebrows knitted. 'What about men and their problems?' Now it was

Carol Shields's turn to be confused. 'Although, on second thoughts,' the Duke continued reflectively, 'there isn't much to say, is there? They've only got one and that's women!'

$\mathcal{A}$t a huge reception at the Royal Academy a few years ago for people from the Arts, Prince Philip was annoyed by the sparseness of the composer Simon Bainbridge's beard, especially when compared to his lovely luxuriant hair. He thought the man should do something about it. 'Why don't you go the whole hog?' he barked.

$\mathcal{M}$eeting dancers after performances at the Ballet Rambert, Princess Margaret liked to express her appreciation in unusually frank ways. Once her hands brushed the chest of a stunningly beautiful Hungarian male dancer. He conceived an equally powerful fascination for the turquoises which adorned her bosom and neck. 'What beautiful turkeises!' he exclaimed, fingering them. They stood admiring each other in this manner for some while. Bystanders were astonished.

Visiting a school of which she was Patron, Princess Margaret was introduced to the biology teacher. She screwed up her face. 'Isn't that all those nasty things in jars?' Next in the line was the history teacher. 'Ah, that's more like it,' she said. No problems with tuning in here. She was a part of history, after all.

Lunching at the Grocers' Company in 1999, the Queen Mother mopped up the little bowl of Belgian chocolates that had been provided for each guest well before the main course. Well, why not?

In the 1970s and 1980s, the film director John Schlesinger made quite a thing of being gay. When the Queen invested him with a CBE and said, of the ribbon she was putting round his neck, 'We must make sure we get it on *straight*,' he was convinced that this was her way of showing gay solidarity. Who knows – maybe it was.

During their 1957 visit to Rhodesia, the Queen Mother and Princess Margaret remained composed when a burly, choleric-looking District

Commissioner curtsied to them by mistake. But later, back at the Mine guesthouse in Ndola, where they were staying, a policeman came across them doing a very expert imitation of the episode, with the Queen Mother giving an excellent impression of the blustering, outsize Commissioner.

*I*n Australia on the Coronation Tour, the Duke of Edinburgh found a way of keeping himself amused on long car journeys. If they passed a pub, he would make a point of waving to those who, after they'd staggered out to catch a glimpse, were obviously more dependent than usual on the lamppost for support. They would try to wave back and immediately fall over.

How Much Does it Cost?

*K*enneth Clark, otherwise known as Lord Clark of Civilisation, complained of the facilities at Windsor Castle in the 1940s. The only telephone was in a corridor surrounded by hordes of eavesdropping footmen. But at least the guest bedrooms were better than might be provided by a Communist regime.

*I*n 1963, the Queen wrote to Sir Hardy Amies: 'Thank you for your note with the account warning me to beware the cost of the pink embroidered evening dress before I actually read it. It was quite a shock . . . I fear that in future I will be unable to order dresses that are so expensive . . . I am sure that you will understand!' Well, she did try, but by 1978, it seems to have been back to square one. Sir Hardy once again warned the Queen in advance that a particular dress was rather costly. Fortunately their relationship was exceptionally friendly, and Her Majesty wrote jokingly, 'Thanks for your enormous bill, which it will take some time to pay!' before going on to order more dresses for the Gulf Visit. 'I'm told "no bare flesh" is the main concern.'

While she was sitting for her portrait one day, the Queen observed through the window a minor accident between a taxicab and a private car. She gave a blow by blow account: the laborious examination of the damage, the exchange of addresses and so on. 'In the meantime,' she said, 'the clock ticks up and the poor thing inside the taxicab will have to pay.'

After the frequent school-style fire drills that were necessary at Sandringham before it was brought up-to-date, the Queen liked the firemen to be given beer. On one occasion, on being told that they had drunk six dozen bottles, she raised her eyebrows. 'I dread to think what they would drink if there were a real fire.'

The Queen displays her Christmas cards on an old wooden clothes-horse.

*W*hen Prince Charles moved into Highgrove he had just his valet and a policeman to help him. After a day of lugging boxes and pieces of furniture, they wondered what they would eat. The valet managed to rustle up Eggs Florentine on a primitive stove. They ate this on their knees in front of the TV.

*I*n 1982, the Queen wrote to Sir Hardy Amies indicating that she wouldn't be able to have any new clothes for some time. Her letter ends wistfully: 'Of course, if you see any nice materials – think of me!!'

*M*embers of the public visiting Sandringham will have noticed the prevalence of hard-wearing upholstery in shades of oatmeal, biscuit and hay. Asking an upholsterer in South London to re-cover a sofa, the Queen's only instruction was, 'Make it match the picture behind it.' She supplied a photograph. Later on, the upholsterer wrote to complain that she had omitted to pay the VAT. For many years he kept the letter of apology from the Queen about the VAT framed on his wall.

*T*he Queen remarked to Annigoni on the poor state of the curtains in the Yellow Drawing Room where they had their sittings. She must get something done about them. But 15 years later another artist, Michael Noakes, painting the Queen in the same room, observed that the grand scheme for new curtains had only got as far as fabric samples, which were lying about.

*I*n 1971, the Queen wrote in person to Sir Hardy Amies to ask him to help her solve a little bureaucratic wrangle she was involved in. 'I meant to ask but stupidly forgot,' she began. Could he kindly itemise his bill a little more exactly as 'I cannot get the Privy Purse to accept my word for the Purchase Tax, as the item is not put separately on the account'? Even the Sovereign cannot escape the quibbling of the money people.

$\mathcal{E}$stée Lauder, the cosmetics tycoon, was not famed for being slow in coming forward. She built up her empire by stopping women in the street and plastering her products all over them before they knew what was happening. She was lucky not to get done for assault. At a party in the South of France, she announced her intention of introducing herself to the main guest, Princess Margaret. Her companions were appalled, knowing full well that you must never impose yourself upon Royalty. But they could do nothing to restrain her. They rather dreaded her mood when she came back after the inevitable snub. But they need not have worried. Estée returned in triumph. 'Oh, it was fantastic,' she exclaimed. 'She was out of *everything*!'

$\mathcal{P}$rincess Margaret ordered the very best sherry glasses in large quantities from the General Trading Company, a grand retail outlet in Sloane Street. She returned them the next day, not even washed up.

$\mathcal{T}$he Queen was sitting for Annigoni one day when the Welch Regiment went by the window with a goat. It was their mascot. The Queen complained that they were getting through too many goats; it was expensive. The soldiers were giving the goats excessive numbers of cigarettes. But the doctor had said two cigarettes a day was as much as a goat could stand. This must not be exceeded. Annigoni felt as though he was drunk.

Outrage at the 2002 Golden Jubilee! Turn-ups with morning coats? What were Princes William and Harry thinking of? Well, if you must know, they were economising by wearing their school trousers, which, because they were pinstriped, were ideal. The oddity of the turn-ups (a unique Eton feature) would just have to be overlooked. Prince William had in fact left Eton some time before the Jubilee so his thrift is even more to be applauded.

Lady Cynthia Colville, lady-in-waiting to Queen Mary, noticing one day that the King and Queen were not about, took the opportunity to nip into King George's bedroom. She wanted to find out how hard his bed was. Her methods were thorough. She jumped up and down on it. It was like jumping on the floor, she reported afterwards.

Queen Mary was disturbed to hear that her son, the Prince of Wales, was having new curtains. She forged into his apartments one day when he was out – with her tape measure. Her instinct was right. The reckless boy had ordered six yards too much material. And the fabric was far too expensive anyway. She selected a cheaper one.

After the War, Crawfie was in a fix. What with shortages and high prices she didn't know how she was going to get curtains and loose covers for her new grace-and-favour cottage. But Queen Mary came to the rescue. 'I know a very good man in the Fulham Road,' she said. 'He's very cheap.' There and then, she wrote the name and number on a card and gave it to the governess.

When he was living at York House, Prince Charles suffered the indignity of a drawing room that would accommodate only seven and a hallway where there was barely room for two people to stand side by side. As he greeted kings and presidents, the Prince enjoyed only a two-inch clearance between his nose and his visitor's.

*I*n the 1970s, Sandringham was shut down for several years for modernisation. The Queen decided that in the meantime the Court would reside at Wood Farm on the estate. This was an excellent plan, the only drawback being that Wood Farm is a four-bedroomed farmhouse. When they came to stay, Princess Anne and her husband had to bring a caravan, which they connected to the electricity through the kitchen window. When the Governor-General of Australia made a formal visit, he had to enter the house through the kitchen (there was no front door to speak of) and wait there until the Queen was ready, while the chef carried on chopping and whisking. Certain functionaries began to look a little redundant. The chef ended up having to answer the telephone. As he called up to the Queen's page, 'Princess Margaret for the Queen, Mr Bennett,' a familiar voice would ring out: 'I heard that.'

The sympathy between the Queen Mother and Norman Hartnell was legendary, oiled, it has to be said, by her high disregard for expense. But when it came to fur trimmings she showed an unexpected economising side. He did find it rather frustrating when, after he completed an outfit, his Royal client would suddenly turn up with a box of fur bits cut off old coats and dresses, insisting they be recycled.

The Queen Mother thought it would be less bother if, on her visits to the Bruton Street salon of Norman Hartnell, she came in by the back entrance. But the couturier complained that it was a terrible bind getting the dustbins spruced up and so forth.

Norman Hartnell had a very splendid salon full of priceless objects. But for the private visits of the Queen Mother he thought he ought to provide something more secluded. A little inner office was selected. It needed doing up but he wasn't going to spend a lot of money since she didn't come *that* often. His decorator, Kenneth Partridge, found a cheap black marbled wallpaper and six chandeliers from Woolworths. The Queen Mother loved the chandeliers and said they would be perfect for the Castle of Mey. She wasn't a bit put off by the Woolworths aspect.

*T*he Queen kept her Frederick Fox black 'Cenotaph' hat going for ten years.

*W*hen the Queen ordered long dresses out of respect for Islamic tradition for her State Visit to the Gulf States in 1979, she said to Hardy Amies, 'Do make sure they'll convert easily into dinner dresses for when I get back home.'

*B*ut sometimes economy goes out of the window. In the 1960s, the Queen got into a bidding war with Roy Strong, then Director of the National Portrait Gallery, for a miniature of Elizabeth I. 'I won by paying more,' the Queen said.

*Q*ueen Mary found that it saved time and effort to have her customary false front of hair sewn into her hat. This operation was carried out in Great Portland Street.

*W*hen Princess Elizabeth was a teenager, it was discovered that two frocks could be made for her out of one of her mother's.

*T*he Queen was glued to the TV during the Moon landing of 1969, until, that is, her set broke down.

*O*n one occasion the Royal Household were leaving Balmoral at the end of the holidays. The ordeal of packing up was at last over and a considerable procession of staff, luggage and Royal persons set off down the drive. Why then the sudden halt? Why was the cavalcade turning back towards the Castle? It turned out that the Queen had seen a light on in one of the windows and was determined to investigate.

'Oh, do grow up, Mummy!' the Queen would exclaim when the Queen Mother proposed yet another outrageous extravagance.

Passing on a horrifying bill from her racing manager, Peter Cazalet, which the Queen had kindly undertaken to pay, the Queen Mother scrawled 'Oh dear!' on the bottom of it.

George V always claimed that the winnings from his horses were what bankrolled his stamp collection. But on his death, his stamp collection was discovered to be one of the most valuable in the world. How could this be when his horses had brought in only the odd few hundred here and there in prize money?

Our Real Friends

*I*n 1962, Sir Hardy Amies's Christmas present to the Queen was a toy kangaroo, which wore a tiara and carried a bouquet. The Queen was thrilled and gave it pride of place on the piano at Sandringham. A few Christmases later, the kangaroo acquired a friend in the form of a magnificent lion, with which Prince Andrew, aged 2, was unimpressed. The Queen reported to Sir Hardy that her family had been dimwitted about which country's flag the lion was bearing. By 1968, there was an astonishing zoo on top of the drawing-room piano, with a hairy dog, a poodle and a dachshund added to the original collection. These last caused some upset to the real dogs. The Queen's puppy was paralysed with horror by the hairy dog, and the toy dachshund and the real dachshund did not get on at all.

*P*rincess Anne's bull terrier, Dotty, who attacked a member of the public in Windsor Great Park in

April 2002, has caused her Royal owner trouble in more ways than one. Guests at Gatcombe Park some years ago were assembled in the drawing room before dinner when an unpleasant smell became noticeable. All the men began guiltily to examine their shoes, afraid that they had trodden in something. But the truth was that Dotty had had an accident by the fireplace. Princess Anne summoned a maid, who wearily assessed the apparently familiar situation and returned with a large roll of kitchen paper. The Princess meanwhile had embarked on a sort of elaborate Aesop's fable of Russian origin about a bird which threw its pursuer, a bear, off the scent by landing in some poo but then went and spoilt it all by boasting so loudly of its escape that the bear found it and ate it anyway. Thus was this distressing domestic episode expertly made light of.

*A*nnigoni used to get very het-up if he felt his Royal portraits weren't turning out well. Once, he kicked one of the Queen Mother's corgis (fortunately she was not present) and it slid across the floor and collided with a grandfather clock, which promptly sprang into life, having not worked for years.

'*I*'m sure Aureole will win,' was the Queen's disconcerting reply to a lady-in-waiting who had asked Her Majesty if she was nervous. The courtier had meant about the forthcoming Coronation, not a horse race.

*R*ecently the Queen revealed her strategy if one of her corgis has an uncontrollable fit of barking. She carries 'mixer biscuit things' in her pocket. From time to time they work. She'd also like the dogs to beg for titbits with one paw outstretched. 'I'm sure they'll learn. Eventually,' she said.

*I*n the 1970s, the Prince of Wales's valet took his master's Labrador, Harvey, for a walk in the garden of Buckingham Palace, having first checked that the coast was clear, that is, that the Queen was not in the garden at the time. Needless to say, the first thing he sees in the distance is the small headscarfed figure. He takes avoiding action. But, proceeding down another path, there she is again. He turns off abruptly, but rounding a corner . . . sure enough, it's her . . . He turns back. But she follows. He can't shake off Her Majesty. Just as he's about to run back into the Palace, the Queen is upon him and speaking: 'I wanted to see how Harvey's getting on. I bred him, you know.' By this time she was a little out of breath.

'We don't shoot owls, do we?' the Queen said to a novice gun at Sandringham who had made an unfortunate mistake.

It's lucky the Queen reads the papers carefully, because at Christmas 2000 she saw in the *Observer* that a centre for retired racehorses at Okehampton in Devon was threatened with closure. Fifteen horses would have to be shot if no home could be found for them. She at once contacted Andrew Parker Bowles, chairman of a charity that could release money to save the centre. 'It was a very kind gesture and in the spirit of Christmas,' the owner said.

*B*efore she was married, the Queen Mother, then Elizabeth Bowes Lyon, was returning from a dance in her father's carriage. When it ground to a halt and showed no sign of moving off again, she asked the coachman what the matter was. 'It's just the 'orse, ma'm. He's having a little sleep.' The Strathmores were none too well off and economised with elderly horses.

*D*uring the War, a frightened terrier bolted down a hole in the East End during an air-raid. All day it was there, the owner standing by, weeping. Nobody could do a thing – until, that is, the Queen Mother, then Queen, came along and said, 'I've got a way with dogs.' She crouched down in the dust and had it out in a jiffy.

*T*he Queen Mother made sure nobody was left out when she fed her dogs dog-chocolate drops. She would say, 'One for you, and one for you.' When every dog had had one, she popped one into her own mouth. 'And one for me.'

*I*n 2000 there was a ridiculous fuss because the Queen was seen by some ignorant journalists wringing the neck of a pheasant that had been shot but was still alive. She was of course doing exactly the right thing in ending the bird's suffering and showing considerable skill and pluck while she was about it. 'Pity she couldn't do the same for Tony Blair,' quipped one onlooker who hadn't quite got the point.

'I don't think they backed a winner,' the Queen Mother remarked of a gloomy painting by Sickert of George V and his racing manager at the 1927 Grand National.

It was fortunate that the Queen didn't notice when Cecil Day-Lewis, Poet Laureate, mistook one of her corgis for a footstool. Mistreatment of her animals is just about the only thing that causes her to lose her cool.

George V's parrot was called Charlotte. She flew free in the dining room. The King was nifty at moving the mustard pot so that Queen Mary wouldn't notice if Charlotte should happen to poo from the air onto the tablecloth.

$\mathcal{A}$ little-known aspect of the man-in-Queen's-bedroom affair is that once the culprit, Michael Fagin, had at last been restrained by the footman, the Queen had great difficulty in keeping her pack of six corgis off him. Perhaps all the security equipment and protection officers surrounding the Queen are really rather redundant.

All in Good Taste

*W*hat was the Queen up to at the Royal Variety Performance in November 2001? In the interval she was doing her lipstick and being rather secretive about her conversation with the head of ITV. 'There are going to be some good programmes on in the New Year,' she announced, looking, according to Gyles Brandreth, who was present, 'as if someone had told her something preposterous'. The Duke of Edinburgh tried to get more out of her, but she wouldn't let on, perhaps on account of Brandreth lurking nearby. So what were these

programmes she was so looking forward to? Well
... wait for it ... ITV's top billing for January
2002 was *Footballers' Wives*! Right up her street.

*T*he Waterloo Room may have been renamed the
Music Room to avoid reopening old wounds
when President Chirac dined there during a State
Visit in November 2004. But the French Head of
State, a well-known opera lover, was not spared
the ghastly agony of a special performance of *Les
Misérables* after dinner.

*H*aving some inkling of the Queen's dislike of
opera and ballet, an overfamiliar minister once
asked how she had borne up during a gala performance. 'Not so loud,' she muttered, reproving
the minister but not exactly denying that she
might have had an ordeal.

*A*t Sandringham, the Queen Mother and Noël
Coward sang 'My Old Man Said Follow the Van'
with exceptional verve.

$\mathcal{A}$ favourite Royal canapé is two cheese biscuits fixed together with cheese paste and topped with chopped ham in béchamel sauce. Delicious.

'$\mathcal{U}$gh! Horrible slimy stuff!' This was the Queen Mother's view of smoked salmon.

$\mathcal{F}$lowers not liked by the Queen Mother – golden rod, African marigolds, Calceolarias.

$\mathcal{L}$ord Carnarvon offered some rare Madeira of 1836 to Princess Margaret. She thought it tasted just like petrol and said so.

$\mathcal{T}$he Queen's description of a wrestling match she had enjoyed on television bordered on a re-enactment when she began to stamp and heave and pretend to hurl herself against the ropes. This was not the camped-up American wrestling we know today but the old-fashioned, more sober kind that used to be shown on ITV on Saturday afternoons. But still, hardly the sport of Kings, let alone Queens.

The Queen caused a sensation at the 1979 Royal Command Performance – she rocked along to 'Rock Around the Clock', performed live by Bill Haley and the Comets. Afterwards she congratulated the singer: 'It took me back to the days of my youth.'

In 1954 Noel Coward attended an amateur performance of *The Frog* by Edgar Wallace in which Princess Margaret had a substantial part. He was most unimpressed; and wrote in his diary that the worst of it was the unwarranted self-satisfaction of the upper-crust cast. Afterwards, Princess Margaret had triumphantly consumed champagne and foie gras in the dressing room. When Coward's diary was published after his death, Princess Margaret knocked the whole thing to the boundary with superb aplomb: 'I don't like foie gras,' she said.

Kenneth Clark, Lord Clark of Civilisation, found himself being frog-marched into being Surveyor of the King's Pictures by George V.

'Come and work for me,' he barked.

'I wouldn't have time to do the job properly.'

'What is there to do?'

'Well, sir, the pictures need looking after.'
'There's nothing wrong with them.'
'But people write letters asking about them.'
'Don't answer them.'

During the California visit of 1983, the Queen's outfit for disembarking from *Britannia* in a howling gale was much criticised. It made her look like a cross between a downmarket pearly queen and a nurse. Hearing of the fuss, the Queen said, 'Stupid people. There was nothing wrong with it.'

George VI confessed that he was confused by the labels on paintings, never being sure which referred to the sitter and which the artist.

John Piper did a dramatic series of pictures of Windsor Castle in his characteristically turbulent style, heavy and dark. 'I see you've been unfortunate with the weather,' George VI remarked.

*E*veryone admired Charles Sims's portrait of George V for the way it showed his graceful legs and out-turned feet. It was agreed that these features had never been so expertly celebrated before. But the King was furious. He ordered that the picture be fetched back from America and incinerated. He thought it made him look like a ballet dancer.

In the Cradle

*W*inston Churchill was prophetic. On meeting the 2-year-old Queen, then Princess Elizabeth, he said, 'She has an air of authority and reflectiveness astonishing in an infant.' This was before anyone had thought of her being Queen. Regality was manifest from the pram. At Windsor the officer in charge of the guard felt compelled to approach the baby's carriage. 'Permission to march off, ma'am.' A little mittened hand was seen to rise and a charming cotton bonnet gravely to nod. Permission was granted.

*E*very morning, Princess Elizabeth kept in touch with her grandfather King George V by waving from her house in Piccadilly while he, in nautical fashion, observed her through binoculars at Buckingham Palace.

The Queen was 5 when her new nanny, the traitor Crawford as it happened, was brought into the nursery to be introduced. It was bedtime and the little girl was busy driving a team of horses around the park. She had rigged up her dressing-gown cord as reins. She only had time to ask Miss Crawford why she had no hair.

Should the occasion require fighting, the little Princesses adopted different styles. Lilibet swung a left hook, while Margaret Rose got up close in order to be in a better position to bite.

Miss Crawford's great battle to get the little Princesses to stop biting their nails was not helped by the example of the Prime Minister, Neville Chamberlain, who bit his too.

The little Princesses' life-saving certificates were lost during the Blitz.

Early on, Princess Elizabeth acquired the right style of Royal conversation. But sometimes the content was awry. Aged about 7, she addressed

Ramsay MacDonald with aplomb. 'I saw you in *Punch* this morning, Mr MacDonald, leading a flock of geese.'

*U*nderneath the magnificent dress that Princess Elizabeth wore to her father's Coronation in 1937, she had short socks and battered knees like any other child.

*I*f the air-raid siren went off in the night, the nurse Alla preferred that the little Princesses should be blown to smithereens by a bomb than that they should go to the shelter, which was a dungeon at Windsor full of beetles, not properly dressed.

'*L*ook at her lovely pink bottie!' exclaimed Queen Mary on coming across a baby god-daughter at bath time. Never again did Queen Mary so dramatically abandon her customary regality.

$\mathcal{T}$he first Royal trans-Atlantic phone call took place in 1939. The King and Queen were on tour and the Princesses Elizabeth and Margaret were at St Paul's Walden Bury. They concluded the conversation by holding one of the Queen's corgis up to the receiver and causing it to bark by giving it a little nip.

'$\mathcal{I}$'ve had some filthy meals from there – you know: children,' the Queen Mother remarked as she wafted past 'Y Bwthyn Bach' in the late 1970s. She referred to the two-thirds-sized cottage given to the little Princesses by the people of Wales in 1932 and equipped with functioning gas cooker and refrigerator, as well as a packet of Epsom Salts – essential for consumers of the Princesses' efforts in the kitchen. Princess Elizabeth was given cooking lessons, but in those days she was more devoted to dusting and tidying. Indeed, she prepared for her parents' return from a six-week tour of America in 1939 by giving the little house a thorough turn-out.

$\mathcal{P}$rincess Anne disgraced herself in church at the age of 3. When, among the prayers for the Royal Family, she heard, 'Charles, Prince of Wales,' she wished to throw further light. 'Duke of Corn-flakes!' she shouted out.

On the night before the Coronation, the Queen combined her State and domestic duties admirably. She went to say goodnight to Prince Charles, aged 4, wearing her crown. She was practising for the big day by wearing it about the house.

Intimate Moments

At the end of a sitting with Annigoni, the Queen looked at the unfinished work: 'One doesn't know oneself,' she said.

In 1990 Sir Hardy Amies retired and the Queen had to face a new couturier. Fortunately, as she told a friend, she found the new man, Mr Fleetwood, not a bit intimidating. She could be as difficult as she liked over changing the designs at a late stage. What's more, Mr Fleetwood was on friendly terms with Frederick Fox, the hat maker. All three of them could get together and have a good laugh about her hats.

The Coronation was an extraordinarily solemn and magnificent occasion, relieved only at the very end, when the Duke of Edinburgh, reunited with the Queen at the door of the Abbey, inquired of her new crown, 'Where did you get that hat?'

The Queen Mother and Norman Hartnell enjoyed a telepathic understanding. During fittings she only had to murmur, 'A little?' or even just, 'Perhaps . . .' to get the message across – that more flounces, gatherings and trimmings were to be added to the garment in question.

George V loathing of abroad was confirmed when, on a State Visit to Belgium in 1922, he and Queen Mary, devoted and inseparable, were given rooms at opposite ends of the gigantic Palace of Laeken – because that's what horrid foreign protocol decreed. But the King's homing instinct was such that he got out of his lonely room and groped his way in the dark through miles of unfamiliar gilded corridors, managing somehow to arrive at the Queen's bedroom. She woke up to see 'his dear little face' peeking round the half-opened door.

*W*ord got around soon after she was married that Princess Diana's Royal style was going to be different. At Belville Sassoon, in Pavilion Road, where she went for fittings, she thought nothing of men being in the room while she was dressed in only her underwear. In fact, the fewer clothes she was wearing, the more skittish and delightful she became.

*D*uring a private visit the Queen paid to some friends living in a cathedral city in the south of England, her hosts were mystified when she paused under a tree in their garden and for some minutes seemed to be in a trance. The birds sang, the branches swayed in the breeze. The Queen did not move. Eventually she said, 'You must be able to hear the birds in your house. I'm not allowed trees near any of my homes.'

*W*hat became of the piece of cloth woven by Gandhi and given to the Queen as a wedding present? Did Queen Mary, who feared that it was a loin cloth, get rid of it? No, the Queen keeps it to this day in a drawer in her bedroom at Buckingham Palace.

*D*uring a painting week for members of the Prince of Wales's Institute of Architecture, held at a secret location, some American students badgered and nagged at the Prince to show them his watercolours. There was no doubt that they hoped to sneer. In the end the Prince gave in and opened his portfolio. Stunned silence. The pictures were not only accomplished but original. The shamed students began to mumble their appreciation. And the Prince stood by, blushing boyishly, delighted but at a loss in the face of *sincere* praise – not something Royalty are used to.

*S*eated conspicuously on a gold throne-like chair in St Paul's Cathedral at the start of the Service of Thanksgiving for her Silver Jubilee, the Queen was seen mouthing something to the Duke of Edinburgh, he looking concerned. Fortunately lip-readers were at hand. 'I feel sick,' the Queen was saying. She did look a little green. The peculiar swaying of the Gold Coronation coach, which she hadn't driven in for 25 years, was thought to be to blame. The next time she rode in this uncomfortable coach, on the way to her Golden Jubilee service at St Paul's in 2002, the problem did not seem to arise. Sea-sickness pills, perhaps?

*I*n all the excitement and festivity of the Queen and Princess Margaret's famous excursion into the streets on VE Day, there was one solemn and moving moment. A Dutch serviceman recognised them. Moving away, he said, 'It is a great honour. I shall never forget this evening.'

*T*he Queen told the writer Hammond Innes that when her father allowed her to go out on the streets on VE Day, she had knocked off a policeman's helmet.

The New-look Monarchy

On 27 January 2005, the Queen had to be up in good time at Sandringham because she needed to catch the 10 a.m. commuter service from King's Lynn to King's Cross if she was not to be late for her engagements in London for Holocaust Memorial Day. At the station she gave the impression that she was travelling alone, but in fact a policeman was lurking. He later went up and down the full train, telling the other passengers that it was the Queen's wish that none of them should stand on her account and that there were plenty of empty seats in her carriage. But nobody dared to approach.

*I*n March 2006, an ordinary London taxi drew up outside the Victoria Palace Theatre shortly before curtain-up for *Billy Elliot the Musical*. Well, yes! Big story. Except that squashed into a corner on the back seat (at least six others crammed within) was the Queen. Lucky it's only a short hop from Buckingham Palace. It would be nice to think that their chauffeur hadn't turned up and they'd had to scurry out into the street to hail a cab. But in fact the taxi belongs to the Duke of Edinburgh and he goes round London in it all the time. It's even eco-friendly and runs on liquid petroleum gas.

*T*he stopover at Singapore and the prospect of luxury goods at bargain prices from the fabulous duty-free facilities at Changi Airport are what keep most passengers going on the gruelling flight back to Britain from Australia. Snap for the Queen! In 2002, she disembarked from her British Airways scheduled flight and made a beeline for the Clarins counter, where she pounced on some anti-wrinkle cream with strong sun screen as well as various unguents for the nails and hands.

$\mathcal{T}$he first official visit to a pub by the Queen took place in March 1998. At the Bridge Inn near Exeter, the landlord presented Her Majesty with 24 bottles of a special brew. She said, 'I'm sure the Duke will enjoy them.' She then turned to her attendants: 'Will they go in the boot?'

$\mathcal{I}$n 2002, Piers Morgan, then editor of the *Mirror*, had the nerve to pounce on the Queen at a Buckingham Palace reception and start cross-examining her about David Beckham's foot. Amazingly she didn't freeze him out. Yes, she was worried about him driving his car. That wouldn't help at all. Could she recommend a physio-therapist? Morgan continued outrageously. 'How about my granddaughter, Zara?' the Queen said.

$\mathcal{A}$t Government House, Kingston, Jamaica in 2002, the lights went out just as the Queen was dressing for a State Banquet. Having felt her way down the stairs to the dining room, by then illumi-nated from outside by the lights of well-positioned parked cars, she made an impromptu reference in her speech to the difficulties of putting a tiara on in the dark. But this should not have been too much of a challenge, for her faithful maid of many years, Bobo MacDonald, often spoke admiringly of the Queen's unique abilities, one of which was that she could put her tiara on while going down stairs.

*P*rince William went on a hearty outdoor holiday to East Africa with his student friends in August 2003. He stayed in a cabin with a cement floor and bamboo roof, no electricity or hot water – for £10 a night.

*I*n 2003, somebody had a crackpot idea that Prince William should become a member of White's, the old-guard gentlemen's club in St James's whose members often resemble sides of beef and are about as mobile. The Prince and some of his friends went on a recce. They played snooker. But the outsize Remembrance Day poppy worn by one of them caused outrage in

the smoking room. No more has been heard of this particular scheme.

In December 2003, Camilla Parker Bowles, as she then was, was hostess when some children suffering from cancer came to tea at Clarence House. She offered round the biscuits. 'They're special. They're Duchy of Cornwall,' she said encouragingly. But the children were not impressed. 'Have they all got orange inside them?' one of them inquired. It was not an easy moment for a hostess, but Mrs Parker Bowles proved herself up to it. 'Is it disgusting?' she said. 'Why don't you put it back?' She did not flinch when the half-chewed biscuit was returned to the plate.

The Buckingham Palace staff Christmas party in 2003 certainly reflected the changing times. A lesbian housemaid and her girlfriend caused a sensation with their matching sailor suits and their intimate dancing. Looking on, the Duke of Edinburgh was delighted. Only senior courtiers were po-faced, apparently.

*P*aying his first visit to a school of which he had recently become Patron, Prince Edward let it be known beforehand that he wanted no grand lunch and no unnecessary dignitaries – just the head-teacher and the head of the juniors would be nice. So it was arranged for the lunch to be held in one of the music practice rooms, measuring about 12′ by 8′.

*D*eborah, Duchess of Devonshire went to a dance at Windsor in the late 1990s and didn't think twice about putting on her biggest tiara for dinner. But, horror of horrors, the new-look monarchy! From the Queen down, not a tiara in sight! She slogged through dinner in agony. As soon as the dancing began, she took the wretched thing off and stowed it under a chair, thinking that Windsor was probably the only place where a tiara left lying around wouldn't get nicked.

*R*ay Davies of the Kinks went to collect his CBE at Buckingham Palace in January 2006 and found the Queen, as always, on top of her brief. 'I'm sorry to hear that you were mugged in New Orleans,' she said and added, 'I hope they get the bastards who shot you.'

It's such a shame that nobody believes this story, despite the relentless insistence of Mr Davies that it is true. Why shouldn't Her Majesty update the monarchy in this fashion, if she chooses? Readers of *You Look Awfully Like the Queen* will remember that when a woman hurled abuse after being drenched by the Queen's car as it carelessly crashed through a puddle, Her Majesty remarked, 'I quite agree with you, madam.' 'What did she say?' inquired the Duke of Edinburgh, who had not been paying attention. 'Bastards!' said the Queen.

So there we are.

Abroad

Just thinking about a hot climate, even in the depths of an icy Norfolk winter, is too much for the Queen. In January 1972, at Sandringham, she complained that she got 'hotter and hotter' whenever anyone mentioned the forthcoming six-week Far Eastern Tour.

The Ambassador and Ambassadress to West Germany were concerned by the astonishing inertness of Princess Diana when she visited with Prince Charles early in her marriage. The Ambassadress arranged some visits to kindergartens, having been told the Princess was interested in children, but nothing raised a spark. Every morning Diana would read about herself in the tabloids and then fall asleep. She had not at that stage become what she afterwards became.

*H*earing that the Queen Mother was to pay a private visit to Brittany, her French hosts, knowing how particular the English are in the matter, made inquiries about tea. What kind did Her Majesty prefer? How should it be made? And so on. Word came back from Clarence House: 'Forget about tea! Gin and tonic will do nicely.'

*T*he Duchess of Cornwall need have no qualms about the incident at the National Institute of Pharmaceutical Research in India when she nearly ended up sprawled on the floor because, making to sit down, she failed to notice that a flunkey had helpfully removed the chair. According to Prince Andrew, the same thing happened to the Queen (albeit in the privacy of her own home) and also, many, many years ago, to the Queen Mother when she was Duchess of York. But that isn't the point. True Royalty always assume a chair. It was noted as a difference between Queen Victoria and the parvenu Empress Eugénie. The unfortunate exiled French Empress always glanced nervously, not certain of the chair, the English Queen never did.

*T*he Duchess of Cornwall showed unusual concern for members of the Press during her 2006 Tour of Egypt, Saudi Arabia and India with her husband. She told one foolish young man that he'd get sunstroke if he didn't keep his hat on and she asked another what his hotel was like. He said, 'Pretty horrible.' 'Well, ours hasn't got any electricity,' she replied consolingly.

*O*n a State Visit to steamy Brazil in 1968, the Queen took one look at a magnificent heavy brocade evening dress trimmed with fur, which Sir Hardy Amies had made for her. 'I can't face it,' she said. It was so hot. In fact she'd have been much happier in a bathing suit, as she told the designer on her return.

Sources

Amies, Hardy, *Still Here: An Autobiography*, London: Weidenfeld and Nicolson, 1984

Annigoni, P., *An Artist's Life*, London: W. H. Allen, 1977

Barry, Stephen, *Royal Service*, New York: Macmillan, 1983

Beaton, Cecil, *The Unexpurgated Beaton Diaries*, ed. Hugo Vickers, London: Orion, 2003

Bennett, Alan, *Untold Stories*, London: Faber and Faber, 2005

Birmingham, Stephen, *Duchess: The Story of Wallis Warfield Windsor*, Boston: Little, Brown, 1981

Blunt, Wilfred, *Slow on the Feather*, London: Michael Russell, 1986

Brandreth, Gyles, *Philip and Elizabeth: Portrait of a Marriage*, London: Arrow Books, 2004

Burrell, Paul, *A Royal Duty*, London: Michael Joseph, 2003

Cartland, Barbara, *Barbara Cartland's Year of Royal Days*, Luton: Lennard, 1988

Clark, Kenneth, *Another Part of the Wood*, London: John Murray, 1974

Crawford, Marion, *The Little Princesses*, London: Orion, 2003

Forbes, Grania, *Elizabeth the Queen Mother*, London: Pavilion Books Ltd, 1999

Gladwyn, Cynthia, *The Paris Embassy*, London: Constable, 1986

Grove, Trevor (ed.), *The Queen Observed*, London: Pavilion, 1986

Hall, Sir Peter, *Diaries*, London: Hamish Hamilton, 1983

Healey, Edna, *Part of the Pattern: Memoirs of a Wife at Westminster*, London: Headline Review, 2005

Hibbert, Christopher, *The Court of St James*, London: Weidenfeld and Nicolson, 1977

Lees-Milne, James: *Diaries* (12 vols.), ed. James Lees-Milne and Michael Bloch, London

Liversidge, Douglas, *The Queen Mother*, London: Arthur Baker, 1980

Longford, Elizabeth (ed.), *The Oxford Book of Royal Anecdotes*, Oxford: OUP, 1989

Longford, Elizabeth, *The Queen Mother: A Biography*, London: Granada, 1981

McDowell, Colin, *A Hundred Years of Royal Style*, London: Muller, Blond &White, 1985

Morgan, Piers, *The Insider: The Private Diaries of a Scandalous Decade*, London: Ebury Press, 2005

Pimlott, Ben, *The Queen: Elizabeth II and the Monarchy*, London: HarperCollins, 2001

Rose, Kenneth, *King George V*, London: Phoenix Press, 2000

Rose, Kenneth, *Kings, Queens and Courtiers*, London: Weidenfeld and Nicolson, 1985

Salisbury, Marchioness of, *The Gardens of Queen Elizabeth the Queen Mother*, London: Mermaid Books, 1988

Saumarez Smith, John (ed.), *The Bookshop at 10 Curzon Street: Letters between Nancy Mitford and Heywood Hill 1952–73*, London: Frances Lincoln, 2004

Secrest, Meryle, *Kenneth Clark: A Biography*, London: Weidenfeld and Nicolson, 1984

Vickers, Hugo, *Elizabeth the Queen Mother*, London: Hutchinson, 2005